Licensed exclusively to Top That Publishing Ltd
Tide Mill Way, Woodbridge, Suffolk, IP12 1AP, UK
www.topthatpublishing.com
Text copyright © 2018 Jaclin Azoulay
Illustrations copyright © 2018 Tide Mill Media
All rights reserved
0 2 4 6 8 9 7 5 3 1
Manufactured in Zhejiang, China

Written by Jaclin Azoulay
Illustrated by Fénix

ISBN 978-1-78700-555-6

Hiccup!

Written by Jaclin Azoulay

For my mom Pat, my dad Angelo, my Uncle Owen,
Raz, Inbar, Gai, Daniel, Lia and Oded. With love always.

Peter the piglet was sad.
Everyone seemed to have forgotten it was
his birthday today. No cards, no presents,
just... "**Hiccup!**"—the hiccups.

Mommy Pig and Daddy Pig were very busy. When Peter the piglet asked if he could help, all that came out was, "**Hiccup!**" "Oink! You go off and play!" Daddy Pig told Peter the piglet.

But Peter the piglet was too sad to play, "**Hiccup!**," so he went to visit Cow instead. When Cow heard Peter the piglet's hiccups she said, "Goodness moo!"

Cow told Peter the piglet that the only cure
for hiccups was to drink a glass of her milk...

...while standing on your head.
But it didn't help. **"Hiccup!"**

Poor Peter the piglet! Now he had the hiccups,
no happy birthday, and milk all over him!
"**Hiccup!** Thank you for trying to help, Cow," he said.

Over at the hen house the naughty, pecky, gossipy hens laughed, "Bok, bok, bok, bok, bok!" when they heard Peter the piglet's hiccups. "**Hiccup!**"
"Everyone knows what you cock-a-doodle-do to cure the hiccups!" said Rooster, with a gleam in his eye. "You must juggle some eggs!"

Peter the piglet wasn't so sure, but he didn't want to be rude. He started to juggle the eggs. Splat! Splat! Splat! "**Hiccup!**" Peter the piglet now had hiccups, no happy birthday, milk all down his face, and egg on his head too!

Peter the piglet didn't feel like saying anything to those mean old hens, but he remembered his manners. "**Hiccup!** Thank you for trying to help," he said.

Peter the piglet sat down feeling very sad and alone.
"Mommy Pig! Daddy Pig!" he cried. "I feel like a pancake!
Hiccup!" He looked all around, but he couldn't see
Mommy Pig or Daddy Pig anywhere.

Horse whinnied to Peter the piglet from the field. Peter the piglet trotted over, "**Hiccup!**"
"Don't worry!" said Horse. "The best cure for hiccups is a good old jiggetty-jog. Climb up onto my back!"

Peter the piglet sat on Horse's back and they jigged and jogged and bumped and bounced all around the field.

It was wonderful fun until...

…Horse saw Mole poke his head up and stopped in surprise. Poor Peter the piglet was catapulted through the air. "Wheee! **Hiccup!**"

"Thank you for trying to help, Horse," Peter the piglet said. "But now I have hiccups, no happy birthday, milk all down my face, egg on my head, and straw stuck everywhere! **Hiccup!**"

Duck quacked at Peter the piglet from the pond, where she was teaching her ducklings to swim. "Oh, Peter!" she said. "I heard your hiccups from over here! You frightened my ducklings! Quack!" "Sorry, Duck. **Hiccup!**" said Peter the piglet.

"Don't you know that the surest cure for
hiccups is a splash of cold water?" Duck said.
With that, Duck and all of her ducklings started
splishing and splashing Peter the piglet.

When they had stopped splashing, Peter the
piglet stood and waited. Duck and her ducklings waited.
"Oh!" Peter the piglet said, at last, with a smile.
"I'm clean again! Thank you Duck, thank you ducklings!
My hiccups have…

Hiccup!...still not gone."
Peter the piglet was clean, but he still had
no happy birthday, and he still had the hiccups!

Then Peter the piglet saw Mommy Pig and
Daddy Pig waving to him from the barn, so he
headed over there as fast as he could.

"HAPPY BIRTHDAY PETER!"
Mommy Pig and Daddy Pig and all of
Peter the piglet's friends were in the barn with the
biggest birthday party he had ever seen!

RTHDAY!

And Peter the piglet found out what the nicest possible cure for hiccups is...a surprise!